Reader's Clubhouse

TOO, TOO HOT!

By Judy Kentor Schmauss
Illustrated by Karol Kaminski

Table of Contents

Illustrations on pages 21 and 23 created by Carol Stutz

All inquiries should be addressed to:
Barron's Educational Series, Inc.
250 Wireless Boulevard
Hauppauge, New York 11788
www.barronseduc.com

Library of Congress Catalog Card No.: 2005053586

ISBN-13: 978-0-7641-3285-8
ISBN-10: 0-7641-3285-7

Library of Congress Cataloging-in-Publication Data
Schmauss, Judy Kentor.
Too, too hot! / Judy Kentor Schmauss.
p. cm. - (Reader's clubhouse)
ISBN-13: 978-0-7641-3285-8
ISBN-10: 0-7641-3285-7
1. Temperature—Juvenile literature. 2. Heat—Juvenile literature. I. Title.
II. Series.

QC271.4.S36 2006
536'.5—dc22

2005053586

Date of manufacture: 09/2009
Manufactured by: Kwong Fat Offset Printing Co., Ltd.
Dongguan City, China

PRINTED IN CHINA
9 8 7 6 5

Dear Parent and Educator,

Welcome to the Barron's Reader's Clubhouse, a series of books that provide a phonics approach to reading.

Phonics is the relationship between letters and sounds. It is a system that teaches children that letters have specific sounds. Level 1 books introduce the short-vowel sounds. Level 2 books progress to the long-vowel sounds. This progression matches how phonics is taught in many classrooms.

Too, Too Hot! introduces the short "o" sound. Simple words with this short-vowel sound are called **decodable words.** The child knows how to sound out these words because he or she has learned the sound they include. This story also contains **high-frequency words.** These are common, everyday words that the child learns to read by sight. High-frequency words help ensure fluency and comprehension. **Challenging words** go a little beyond the reading level. The child will identify these words with help from the illustration on the page. All words are listed by their category on page 24.

Here are some coaching and prompting statements you can use to help a young reader read *Too, Too Hot!*:

- **On page 4, "hot" is a decodable word. Point to the word and say:**

  Read this word. How did you know the word? What sounds did it make?

  Note: There are many opportunities to repeat the above instruction throughout the book.

- **On page 16, "chop" is a challenging word. Point to the word and say:**

  Read this word. It rhymes with "hop." How did you know the word? Did you look at the picture? How did it help?

You'll find more coaching ideas on the Reader's Clubhouse Web site: *www.barronsclubhouse.com.* Reader's Clubhouse is designed to teach and reinforce reading skills in a fun way. We hope you enjoy helping children discover their love of reading!

Sincerely,

Nancy Harris

Nancy Harris
Reading Consultant

It is hot.

It is too, too hot.

Bob likes to jog.

It is too hot for Bob.

Lon likes to jump.

It is too hot for Lon.

Don likes to run.

It is too hot for Don.

Pop likes to mop.

It is too hot for Pop.

Dot likes to trot.

It is too hot for Dot.

Mom likes to chop.

It is too hot for Mom.

Is it too hot for me?
No, it is not.

I like it hot a lot!

Fun Facts About The Heat

- The more you exercise, the more you sweat. If you sweat a lot and don't drink plenty of water, you can get *dehydrated.* Being dehydrated can make you sick.

- On July 10, 1913, the temperature in Death Valley, California, was 134° Fahrenheit (56.6° Celsius). That's the hottest day ever recorded in North America.

- We can tell how hot or cold the air is by using a thermometer. On a very cold day, the temperature is about 20° Fahrenheit (6.6° Celsius) and lower. On a very hot day, the temperature is about 90° Fahrenheit (32.2° Celsius) and higher.

• Here are some important temperatures to know:

Water freezes when it is cooled to 32° Fahrenheit (0° Celsius).

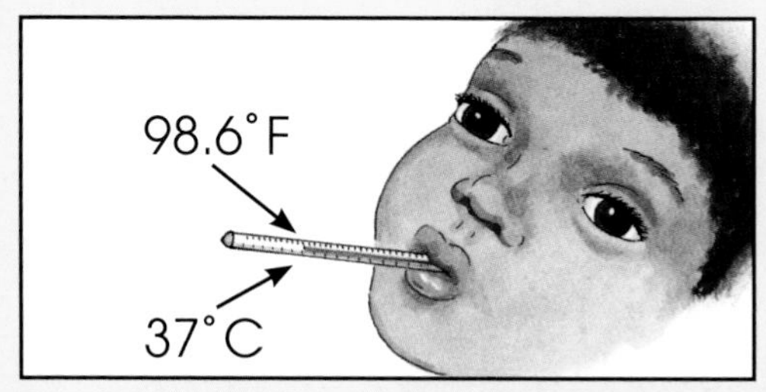

Your normal body temperature is 98.6° Fahrenheit (37° Celsius).

Water boils when it is heated to 212° Fahrenheit (100° Celsius).

Animal Fan

Let your favorite animal keep you cool on a hot day.

You will need:

- corrugated cardboard
- 8 1/2 x 11-inch scrap paper
- pencil
- safety scissors
- colored construction paper
- glue
- popsicle stick
- markers or crayons
- googly eyes (optional)

1. Draw the outline of your favorite animal's face on the scrap paper. Cut out the face to use as a pattern.

2. Trace around the pattern on a piece of construction paper and on the cardboard. Make sure to hold the cardboard so that the ribs/lines are vertical (standing up).

3. Glue the construction paper to the cardboard.

4. Create the animal's features (eyes, nose, mouth, ears, whiskers) out of other pieces of construction paper. If desired, use the googly eyes. Glue the features onto the animal's face.

5. Put a little bit of glue on one end of the popsicle stick. Push the popsicle stick into the inside of the cardboard, between the ribs.

6. Let the glue dry for a little while.

7. Have fun letting your animal keep you cool!

Word List

Challenging Words	chop	
Short O Decodable Words	Bob Don Dot hot jog Lon lot Mom mop	Pop trot
High-Frequency Words	a for I is it jump like likes me no not run	to too